Anonymous

Leisure Hour Work for Ladies

containing instructions for flower and shell work, antique, Grecian and

theorem painting, botanical specimens, cone work

Anonymous

Leisure Hour Work for Ladies
containing instructions for flower and shell work, antique, Grecian and theorem painting, botanical specimens, cone work

ISBN/EAN: 9783337391812

Printed in Europe, USA, Canada, Australia, Japan

Cover: Foto ©Andreas Hilbeck / pixelio.de

More available books at **www.hansebooks.com**

ĽEISURE HOUR WORK

FOR LADIES:

CONTAINING

INSTRUCTIONS FOR FLOWER AND SHELL WORK, ANTIQUE, GRECIAN
AND THEOREM PAINTING, BOTANICAL SPECIMENS, CONE WORK,
ANGLO-JAPANESE WORK, DECALCOMAINE, DIAPHANIE, LEATHER
WORK, MODELLING IN CLAY, TRANSFERRING, CRAYON
DRAWING, PHOTOGRAPH COLORING, &c., &c.

NEW YORK
FRANK M. REED,
PUBLISHER.

LEISURE-HOUR WORK FOR LADIES.

To Preserve and Restore Flowers.—Flowers may be preserved in a fresh state for a considerable time, by keeping them in a moist atmosphere. A flat dish of porcelain had water poured into it: in the water a vase of flowers was set; over the whole a bell-glass was placed, with its rim in the water. The air that surrounded the flowers being confined beneath the bell-glass, was kept constantly moist with the water that rose into it in the form of vapor. As fast as the water was condensed it ran down the sides of the bell-glass back into the dish; and if means had been taken to inclose the water on the outside of the bell-glass, so as to prevent its evaporating into the air of the sitting-room, the atmosphere around the flowers would have remained continually damp. We recommend those who love to see plenty of fresh flowers in their sitting-rooms in dry weather to adopt this method. The experiment can be tried by inverting a tumbler over a rosebud in a saucer of water. Another method by which some flowers may be preserved for many months, is to carefully dip them, as soon as gathered, in perfectly limpid gum-water, and after allowing them to drain two or three minutes, to set them upright, or arrange them in the usual manner of an empty vase. The gum gradually forms a transparent coating on the surface of the petals and stems, and preserves their figure and color long after they have become dry and crisp. Faded flowers may be generally more or less restored by immersing them half way up their stems in very hot water, and allowing them to remain in it until it cools, or they have recovered. The coddled portion of the stems must then be cut off, and the flowers placed in clean cold water. In this way a great number of faded flowers may be restored, but there are some of the more fugacious kinds on which it proves useless.

To Preserve Flowers in Sand.—Get the finest and whitest of river or lake sand, wash it so clean that the water in flowing from it will be pure as if from the well. Heat it very hot, and while hot mix it thoroughly with stearic acid in the proportion of one pound of the latter to one hundred pounds of sand. . Let it cool. Take a small common sieve and nail boards under the bottom to prevent the sand from running through; place enough sand in the sieve to hold the flowers in position—not covering them; then with a sheet of paper twisted in the form of a cone or funnel, carefully let the sand pass through it—between, around, and over the flowers; cover about half an inch. Set by the stove or in some warm place, where the sand will be kept at a temperature of seventy degrees Fahrenheit. When they have remained sufficiently long, remove the boards carefully from the bottom and let the sand run out, leaving your flowers preserved in perfection. The only difficulty is to know when the process is complete, different plants differing in the time required, those with thick leaves and petals needing more than light ones. No exact rule can be given on this point. Seven hours are sufficient for some, while others require twelve, and even more. Experience alone can determine this. It is best always for a beginner to experiment with a single plant at a time at fir t. When he has succeeded with a certain variety, and noted the time required, he can proceed to others, and in a short time become versed in this art. It should be mentioned that the flowers for this purpose should be picked dry—say midday, after the dew is evaporated.

To Preserve Cut Flowers.—Add to the water a little of a solution of carbonate of ammonia and a few drops of phosphate of soda. The effect of this in giving the flower a deeper color and a stronger appearance is quite wonderful; and by cutting off every other day about one half inch of the stems of the flowers with a sharp knife, they may be kept as long as their natural life would last.

To Preserve Plants with their Natural Appearance.—Fine white quartz sand is heated to about two hundred degrees Fahrenheit, in an iron pot, and by stirring, some stearic acid and spermaceti, each in the proportion of half a drachm for every five pounds of sand, incorporated with it. Taken from the fire, the whole is thoroughly mixed and used as follows: A cigar-box with a draw lid, with the bottom knocked out, is inverted, and a coarse piece of wire gauze placed inside over the lid, which now forms the bottom. The bottom and this sieve are then covered by a layer of the prepared sand; the plants, properly trimmed, are placed on this sand, and completely imbedded in more of it, so as to keep them properly in position. The box, covered with paper, is then placed in a room in which a temperature of one hundred to one hundred and ten degrees Fahrenheit is kept up, in which the plants will soon be dried. When this point is reached, the lid of the box is drawn, which causes all the sand to fall out, leaving the dried plants on the gauze.

To Preserve Autumn Leaves.—The beautiful colors of the leaves at this season are indicative of the first stage of decay. If rapidly dried, the process may be arrested and the fine colors preserved. Dry as quickly as possible, by putting the leaves between folds of any very absorbent paper, and change frequently—as often as once a day. A warm flat-iron judiciously used will help the drying, but overheating will spoil all. When the leaves are quickly and thoroughly dried, they will retain their colors for some months. In making up ornamental work, the leaves should have a light coat of boiled linseed-oil. This brings out the color, and gives a more natural appearance than varnish of any kind. For fastening them to cardboard or any other support, glue is best. Do not oil the under sides of the leaves, as this will prevent the glue from adhering.

Anglo-Japanese Work.— This is an elegant and easy domestic art. Take yellow, withered leaves, dissolve gum, get mixed black paint, and some copal varnish, etc. Any articles may be ornamented with these simple materials—an old work-box, tea-caddy, fire-screen, flower-pot, etc. Select perfect leaves, dry and press them between the leaves of books; rub the surface of the article to be ornamented with fine sandpaper; then give it a coat of fine black paint, which should be procured mixed at a color shop. When dry, rub smooth with pumice-stone; then apply two other coats. Dry; arrange leaves in any order, according to taste. Gum the leaves on the under side, and press them upon their places. Then dissolve some isinglass in hot water, and brush it over the work while the solution is warm; when dry, give three coats of copal varnish, allowing ample time for each coat to dry. Articles thus ornamented last for years, and are very pleasing.

Antique Painting.—Apply with a stiff brush a very thin coat of antique varnish, which will be thoroughly dry in six hours; then apply another coat of the same, thin and very equal and smooth. Allow this to dry one hour or until nearly dry, strongly adhering to the finger when touched, but not sticky. Then put on the engraving (having dampened it thoroughly with warm water, not too wet, absorbing the extra moisture with a cloth or blotter), with the face to the varnished side of the glass; press it gently until every part adheres to the surface· rub carefully with your finger a part of the figure, being sure not to rub through the engraving; after it has dried twelve hours, wet again and rub off all the paper, leaving only the engraving; when again dry, moisten carefully with fine bleached drying-oil. It is then fit for painting. The colors will strike through very freely, as there is no paper left, and will not spot as the Grecian is liable to do. Do not use any turpentine in this style. The directions are the same as for Grecian painting, except more pains should be taken to shade and blend in the colors, to help the shading in the engraving, particularly the flesh-color with the hair.

To Dry Botanical Specimens for Preservation.— The plants you wish to preserve should be gathered when the weather is dry; and after placing the ends in water, let them remain in a cool place till the next day. When about to be submitted to the process of drying, place each plant between several sheets of blotting-paper, and iron it with a large smooth heater pretty strongly warmed, till all the moisture is dissipated. Colors may thus be fixed which otherwise become pale or nearly white. Some plants require more moderate heat than others, and herein consists the nicety of the experiment; but I have generally found that if the iron be not too hot, and is passed rapidly, yet carefully, over the surface of the blotting-paper, it answers the purpose equally well with plants of almost every variety of hue and thickness. In compound flowers, with those also of a stubborn and solid form, some little care and skill are required in cutting away the under part, by which means the profile and forms of the flowers will be more distinctly exhibited. This is especially necessary when the method employed by Major Velley is adopted, viz., to fix the flowers and fruit down securely with gum upon the paper, previous to ironing, by which means they become almost incorporated with the surface. When this very delicate process is attempted, blotting-paper should be laid under every part excepting the blossoms, in order to prevent staining the white paper. Great care must be taken to keep preserved specimens in a dry place, and also to handle them gently; and thus they can be kept a long time, affording a source of great pleasure.

Bouquets of Colored Grass.—The grasses should be gathered while the seeds are green, so that after having been hung in a dry, dark place, a week or two, or until thoroughly dried, the seed will not rattle off when shaken. The finer seeded the grasses the handsomer the bouquets; and yet sprigs of green oats work up tastily. The ingredients required are simple and cheap, viz., Common starch and dry chrome paints of as many colors as you wish; an ounce of each is sufficient for making a good-sized bouquet. Dissolve in cold water three tablespoonfuls of starch; then pour on boiling water until cooked; let cool; arrange upon the table your paints, grasses, and starch. Into the starch dip the sprays required for the several colors; shake, and then brush into the paint of whatever color you wish; shake again, and lay them one side upon a board or convenient place to let remain undisturbed until dry. Serve the sprays for each different color in the same way. When dry, lightly shake off the surplus paint, if any, and then form into bouquets. These, particularly when used in connection with crystallized grasses and put into a nicely made wall-basket, of shield form, and hung upon the wall, or even into a vase, are well worth the "care and trouble" of making.

Cone Work.—Select good clear cones, and dissect some which have handsome, large scales, and brush them clean; lay nice white putty, or a similar adhesive substance, smoothly on your frame; set into this putty whole cones, large and small, in such figures as suit your taste, and fill up the entire groundwork with the scales, lapping one neatly over the other. Cut oval and round frames for light pictures, from bookbinder's pasteboard, and cover with the scales in layers or rows. Scallop the edges with small whole cones, set in large cones surrounded by little ones equidistant, if the frame be broad, and fill in with the scales. When dry, take out those which are not firm, and replace. Add acorns ad libitum. Varnish the whole once or twice. If you wish something nice, go over every part with a fine brush, and leave no varnish standing in drops. Cones can be found by almost any one in an hour's walk through pine woods. Indeed, if one has a taste for the beautiful, and is quick in perception, it is impossible to ramble through wood and fields without finding many curiosities in the shape of mosses, grasses, cones, etc.

To Preserve Fungi.—Take two ounces of sulphate of copper, or blue vitriol, and reduce it to powder, and pour upon it a pint of boiling water, and when cold, add half a pint of spirits of wine; cork it well, and call it "the pickle." To eight pints of water add one pint and a half of spirits of wine, and call it "the liquor." Be provided with a number of wide-mouthed bottles of different sizes, all well fitted with corks. The fungi should be left on the table as long as possible, to allow the moisture to evaporate; they should then be placed in the pickle for three hours, or longer, if necessary; then place them in the bottles intended for their reception, and fill with the liquor. They should then be well corked and sealed, and arranged in order with their names in front of the bottles.

Decalcomaina, or the art of ornamenting China, Glass, Earthenware, Woodenware, Fancy Boxes, Ivory, and Papier-Mache Goods, Japanned Ware, Binding of Books, Fans, Leather Work, etc., etc.— *Directions.* — Cover the picture entirely (taking care not to go beyond the outlines) with a slight coat of fixing varnish; then put the picture on the object to be ornamented, being careful to place it properly at once, in order not to spoil it by moving. The varnish newly applied being too liquid, the picture should be left to dry eight or ten minutes, and placed on the object to be ornamented, when just damp enough to be still adherent. This done, cover the back of the picture with a piece of cloth steeped in water; then, by means of a knife or penholder, rub it all over, so as to fix every part of it; then remove the piece of cloth, and rinse the paper with a paint-brush steeped in water; at the end of a few minutes the paper will come off, leaving the painting transferred. Care must be taken that the piece of cloth, without being too wet, should be sufficiently so for the paper to be entirely saturated. The picture must now be washed with a wet paint-brush, and dried very lightly with some blotting-paper. The ornamented article should, after this, be put near the stove or any other warm place, to make it dry well and to improve the adhesiveness of the pictures. The polishing varnish should not be applied until the next day, keeping the pictures in the meantime carefully out of the dust. The latter varnish should be put on as lightly as possible. If dark-colored objects are to be ornamented, such as bindings of books, Russia leather, leather bags, etc., the picture must first be covered with a mixture of white lead and turpentine, following the outlines of the design and covering it entirely. When this coat is perfectly dry, proceed according to the above instructions. To print on silk, paper, or materials that cannot bear washing after the process, proceed as follows: Cover the picture entirely with a light coat of fixing varnish, and let it dry for an hour or two; then pass a sponge, lightly damped, over the whole surface of the paper, in order to take away the composition which is on it in the blank parts, and which often cleans the material. When the paper is dry, re-varnish the picture, and transfer it on to the material by means of a paper-cutter, avoiding to employ the piece of cloth or anything damp; then, with a paint-brush slightly steeped in water, wet the paper lightly, and leave it a full quarter of an hour on the object before removing it. To remove a spoiled print, rub it with a soft rag imbibed in turpentine. Our readers will at once appreciate the merits of this invention; the facility with which it can be applied, also its numerous applications.

Diaphanie.—This is a process by means of which colored designs may be transferred from the paper on which they are originally printed, for the decoration in colors of glass which is intended to admit light. It is, in fact, a method of glass-staining which costs only a fraction of the expense of the ancient process, produces quite as bold and brilliant effects, is sufficiently durable for all ordinary purposes, and can be practiced by amateurs of either sex at their own homes. That diaphanie fully answers the purpose for which it is mainly intended—the staining of glass—is abundantly proved by the fact that many church windows are colored by means of it, and that they are esteemed quite as telling and beautiful specimens of decoration as those that owe their origin to the old and expensive art. For ordinary purposes the process may be described in a few words. In the first place, designs must be obtained, and these can be got in every variety, and suitable for any size of window or pane. First wet the back, or the uncolored side, with a sponge and cold water, and apply a coating of prepared transferring varnish to the colored surface with a wide camel-hair brush. Then at once apply the cemented side to the glass in the proper position, and press down with a roller. To insure success, two or three sheets of paper should be laid upon the back of the design before the using of the roller is commenced; then begin rolling from the centre outward to the circumference. The work is now to be left until the varnish has become perfectly dry, which it will do in two days. The design has by this time become printed upon the glass, and the next step is to remove the paper from which the design has been transferred. This is done by wetting and gently rubbing with a cloth or sponge. When the paper has been wholly removed, a thin coating of "clearing liquid" is applied to the design, and when this has become perfectly dry, one or two coatings of the "washable varnish" are laid on, and the work is finished. No special knowledge of art is required for the practice of diaphanie. The work is especially suitable for hall and lobby doors and windows, for school and church windows; staircase, study, and other windows in houses where it may be desirable to shut out the prospect of a smoke-dried back yard, or a range of mews. The special advantage of diaphanie is that while imparting a graceful and artistic character wherever used, it does not exclude the light, and it renders blinds unnecessary. It should be specially kept in view that the designs must be transferred before the glass is fitted to the window, and that the colored side is kept inwards. The glass may be cleaned in the usual manner, if ordinary care be taken, as the coatings of "washable varnish" are quite a sufficient protection to the picture.

Gaslight Pictures.— Cut all the white paper close up to the engraving, and place the engraving on the glass, like the Antique Painting; then paint a wreath around the engraving, on the glass, oval shape or round. Make a back-ground by painting the back-board with white paint, and before it dries take white or blue frosting, a pinch at a time, with the fingers, and scatter thickly all over the painted board. When the board is dry, shake off what frosting there is that does not adhere, and save it for the next time. A sufficient quantity will adhere to present the appearance of myriads of diamonds, and is very effective, especially by gaslight. In putting the back-board on the picture in this style, put pasteboard strips or thin wood between the glass and the back to keep the glass from mashing down the frosting.

To Crystallize Grasses.—Pulverize a pound of the best white alum, and dissolve it over a slow fire in a quart of pure soft water. Do not let it boil, and be careful to keep everything out of the solution that would possibly stain it, for the beauty of the grasses depends on the pure whiteness of the crystals. A new earthen bowl is the best dish for the purpose; when the alum is dissolved, let the solution cool down to blood heat; meanwhile arrange your grasses in the bowl and pour the solution over them; cover up and set away for twenty-four hours. Then take them out carefully, dry them in the sun four or five hours, and put them in the vase prepared for them. If you form the grasses, etc., into a bouquet before crystallizing them, procure a glazed earthen jar, suspend the bouquet from a stick laid across the top of the jar; take care that the tops of the grasses are not bent or doubled over, and then pour on the solution, proceeding as above directed. What remains of the alum-water may be re-heated, tinged blue, or purple, or scarlet, by a few drops of dye, and used as before. Of course the same preparation is suitable for all kinds of plants.

Grecian Painting.—Procure a light pine frame, a trifle larger than the engraving: (this need not be of the nicest workmanship—simply four pieces of wood nailed together, to act as a support to the picture while painting); then moisten your engraving with water, and while wet paste it to the frame; dry slowly, not over a fire, and it will become quite smooth and tight; now, moisten again on the wrong side with pure spirits of turpentine, and while wet, with a coat of Grecian varnish on the same side, which continue to apply (keeping damp only, not too wet, or it will filter through in spots), until it is wholly transparent and without spots. If it is found difficult to remove the spots, apply the second coat of spirits, and afterwards the Grecian varnish. When ready to paint, the back will have an even gloss all over it. When perfectly clear it should remain two or three days before painting, which is done on the side that you have varnished, the shading of the engraving serving the same purpose in painting. This process is so simple that a child able to read this can understand it. Varnish the picture but once on the face after it is framed (not before), with outside varnish; this must be put on evenly, and with care that it does not run; have but little in the brush at a time.

To Make a Fac-Simile of a Leaf in Copper.—This beautiful experiment can be performed by any person in possession of a common galvanic battery. The process is as follows: Soften a piece of gutta-percha over a candle, or before a fire; knead it with the moist fingers upon a table, until the surface is large enough to cover the leaf to be copied; lay the leaf flat upon the surface, and press every part well into the gum. In about five minutes the leaf may be removed, when, if the operation has been carefully performed, a perfect impression of the leaf will be made on the gutta-percha. This must now be attached to the wire in connection with the zinc end of the battery (which can easily be done by heating the end of the wire, and pressing it into the gutta-percha), dusted well over with the best black lead, with a camel's-hair brush—the object of which is to render it a conductor of electricity, and then completely immersed in a saturated solution of sulphate of copper. A piece of copper attached to the wire in connection with the copper end of the battery, must also be inserted into the copper solution, facing the gutta-percha, but not touching it; this not only acts as a conductor to the electricity, but also maintains the solution of copper of a permanent strength. In a short time the copper will be found to creep over the whole surface of the gutta-percha, and in about twenty-four hours a thick deposit of copper will be obtained, which may then be detached from the mould. The accuracy with which a leaf may thus be cast is truly surprising. Casts taken in this way delineate every fibre and nerve; in fact, the minutest parts, with the greatest fidelity.

To Take Impressions of Leaves, Plants, Etc.— Take half a sheet of fine wove paper and oil it well with sweet oil; after it has stood a minute or two, to let it soak through, rub off the superfluous oil with a piece of paper, and let it hang in the air to dry; after the oil is pretty well dried in, take a lighted candle, and move the paper over it, in a horizontal direction, so as to touch the flame, till it is perfectly black. When you wish to take off impressions of plants, lay your plant carefully on the oiled paper, lay a piece of clean paper over it, and rub it with your finger equally in all parts for half a minute; then take up your plant and be careful not to disturb the order of the leaves, and place it on the paper on which you wish to have the impression; then cover it with a piece of blotting-paper, and rub it with your finger for a short time, and you will have an impression superior to the finest engraving. The same piece of black paper will serve to take off a great number of impressions. The principal excellence of this method is, that the paper receives the impression of the most minute veins and hairs, so that you obtain the general character of most flowers. The impression may afterwards be colored.

Skeleton Leaves.—Skeleton leaves are among the most beautiful objects in nature; and as they can be arranged either in groups under glass shades, made into pictures, as it were, and hung against the wall, or placed in either blank-books or albums, they come within the means of all, and can be used to decorate the palace or the cottage. The most suitable leaves for the purpose are those from what botanists call exogenous plants, and may be known by the veins of the leaf branching from a central vein or midrib; those from endogenous plants rising from the base and curving towards the apex of the leaf. The object in view is to destroy what may be called the fleshy part of the leaf, as well as the skin, leaving only the ribs or veins. The most successful, and probably the simplest, way to do this is to macerate the leaves in rain-water till they are decomposed. For this purpose, when the leaves are collected they should be placed in an earthenware pan or a wooden tub, kept covered with rain-water, and allowed to stand in the sun. In about a fortnight's time they should be examined, and if found pulpy and decaying, will be ready for skeletonizing, for which process some cards, a camel's-hair brush, as well as one rather stiff (a tooth-brush, for instance), will be required. When all is prepared, gently float a leaf on to a card, and with the soft brush carefully remove the skin. Have ready a basin of clean water. and when the skin of one side is completely removed, reverse the card in the water, and slip it under the leaf, so that the other side is uppermost. Brush this to remove the skin, when the fleshy part will most likely come with it; but if not, it will readily wash out in the basin of water. If particles of the green-colored matter still adhere to the skeleton, endeavor to remove them with the soft brush; but if that is of no avail, the hard one must be used. Great care will be necessary to avoid breaking the skeleton, and the hard brush should only be used in a perpendicular direction (a sort of gentle tapping), as any horizontal motion or "brushing" action will infallibly break the skeleton. Never attempt to touch the leaves or the skeleton in this state with the fingers, as when they are soft their own weight will often break them. A very good way of bleaching the skeletons is to prepare a solution of chloride of lime, which must be allowed to settle, and the clear liquid poured into a basin, in which the skeletons may be put by floating them off the card. It is as well to have half a dozen ready to bleach at once, as they require watching, and if allowed to remain in too long will fall to pieces. From two to four hours will generally suffice to bleach the skeleton of all ordinary leaves, after which they should be washed in several changes of water, and finally left in clean water for half an hour. After the leaf has been sufficiently washed it should be floated on to a card and dried as quickly as possible, care being taken to arrange the skeleton perfectly flat, and as near as possible to the natural shape. This can be done with the assistance of the soft brush. When dry the skeleton should be perfectly white, and should be mounted on dark backgrounds, as black velvet or paper. Well-grown leaves should always be chosen, and be thoroughly examined for flaws before maceration. Leaves containing much tannin cannot be skeletonized by this process, but are generally placed in a box with a number of caddis worms, which eat away the fleshy parts, when the skeletons can be bleached in the usual way. Holly-leaves must be placed in a separate vessel on account of their spines, which would be apt to damage other leaves; they make beautiful skeletons, and are sufficiently strong to be moved with the fingers.

Leather Work.—The materials required are the basil leather, thin skiver leather, a bottle of oak varnish, liquid glue, stiffening, small hammer, veining-tool, brad-awl, scissors, sharp knife, cutting-board, mold (or grapes for large peas), brushes, black-lead pencil, and the frame, bracket, or whatever you wish to ornament. The leather used for general purposes is basil; it should be of an even texture, close grain, free from grease, hard, and of a light color, as the lighter colored takes the oak varnish stain better than the dark. There is a faced basil very attractive to the eye, but unserviceable for many operations where firmness is required; it answers well for rolling into stems when the work is intended to be colored. Lamb-skin and deer-skin may be used in some parts, but in all cases avoid a soft, flabby kind of leather; the skiver leather is used for making grapes, but old kid gloves can take the place of this very well. . . . *For Making the Leaves.* —Select a leaf such as you wish to make; sketch it carefully on pasteboard, and cut it out thin; place a piece of leather in cold water for half a minute (not longer), unless the leather is unusually thick. Take it out of the water and press in a linen cloth until the surface becomes dry. Place it flat upon a smooth board, and place upon it your pasteboard pattern, and draw around it with a fine lead pencil, while the leather is damp; cut out the leaf with a pair of scissors or knife. Small or large leaves may be made in the same way. Vein the leaves with the veining-tool (using it as a lead pencil in drawing upon the smooth side of the leaf; bear heavily where the strong indentations are required and lightly where the finer veins are wanted. Each leaf must now be bent and moulded to suit the position it is to occupy when the work is done; they should now be dried quickly and hardened; this is done by applying a coating of the prepared stiffening. Great care should be taken to cover the edges; a rather large camel's-hair pencil is the best to apply it with; the leaves will soon dry and be ready for the staining. Brush them over with the oak-stain varnish, thinly but evenly; a child's hair-brush is best for this. The stain must not be allowed to lodge in the veined parts, or the veins will appear too black. When the leaves are dry they are ready for use; if they are not dark enough, a second application of the stain will be needed..... *To Make Stems, etc.*—Cut strips of basil one third of an inch wide and as long as the leather will allow; soak thoroughly in water; then roll up, the smooth side out, as round as possible, on a table or other smooth surface. Dry quickly by the fire. If the stems are wanted, very stiff wire should be rolled inside the leather. A prettier effect is produced by cutting the stem and leaf in one piece, and made to look like a vine. .... *To Make Tendrils.*—Tendrils are made the same as stems, using the skiver leather instead of the basil. Take a piece of the prepared tendril the length required for winding; damp it slightly, and immediately wind it around the point of a brad-awl, taking care to secure both ends of the tendril; dry by the fire, and remove from the awl, and a delicately formed tendril will be the result. The stems and tendrils should be hardened and stained in the same way as the leaves..... *Flowers* should be made in as few pieces as possible. Roses, Dahlias, etc., can be formed very prettily; the number of stamens should be carefully observed, and inserted in the middle of the flower, using wire for the stems..... *For Grapes.*—Large-sized round peas are good; for this, cut from your skiver or old kid, rounds of the right size; strain and tie closely over the pea, winding tightly the loose ends of the kid to form a stem; they should be stained and made into clusters; it is necessary to observe, in making the clusters, that the tying should be entirely concealed..... *To Make Acorns.*— Procure some natural acorn-cups;

choose such cups as are perfectly sound; pierce two holes through the bottom of the cup; pass a piece of fine wire through the holes, leaving the two ends long enough to be twisted into a stalk; if the stalk is to be exposed, it must be covered with skiver and made fast with glue. The most correctly formed acorn-tops are those turned in wood, which can be firmly placed in the cup with the aid of glue..... *To Cover a Frame.*—Procure a wood frame the size and form required, taking care to have it made of well-seasoned wood; size it all over with patent size. Leave it for an hour to dry, then apply a coating of oak varnish; stain, and when dry it is ready for use. Commence the process of covering by attaching the stems with small tacks all around in a zig-zag direction. If the vine-pattern frame is selected, cover the wood with four or five gradations of foliage, well arranged, so as to preserve as nearly as possible the natural appearance of the vine. Too great a profusion of grapes should be avoided; one large cluster in each corner (if the frame is square) to hang down over the glass, and give it the appearance of a round frame in the inside, is very handsome.

To Model in Clay.—As an interesting, intellectual occupation for leisure hours, modelling in clay has recently been looked upon, especially by ladies, with growing favor. The occupation is really a cleanly one, though at first it might not be thought so. The clay employed is fine white clay—the clay of which pipes are made—and is readily removed by washing. And though no sensible amateur would willingly set up his modelling apparatus in a drawing-room if he could obtain the use of a room less expensively furnished, yet even here the work may be carried on by an ordinarily careful person without endangering carpet or furniture. Of the noble art of sculpture, modelling is by far the most important part—is the only part, in fact, which exclusively employs the genius of the sculptor himself; for, the subsequent processes of casting and carving in marble are carried out in great part, if not entirely, by workmen and assistants. The tools employed are chiefly those with which nature has furnished us—the fingers and thumbs; and, as clay can be purchased for a mere trifle, the material required in modelling will cost the amateur no more than a very few shillings. In carving we cut down our material to the desired form; in modelling we build up our clay to the required form. The process consists of laying on the clay and smoothing down until gradually the model assumes the full proportions of the object we desire to reproduce. Suppose, then, we have to copy a vase in low relief, from a plaster cast. We place the cast before us; and having provided a slate slab, we draw upon the slab the outline of the cast with a slate pencil. Preserving this drawing as the outline, we commence to lay on the clay, modelling it as we proceed with the fingers. This process is continued until the model projects from the slab precisely as the vase does in the casts; and is, in fact, a fac-simile of it. If the face have no ornamentation upon it—and the simplest possible copy should be selected for a first attempt in modelling—this work may all be done with the fingers. When there is ornamentation, the clay must be laid on cautiously, and worked into form by means of the tools, which are usually made of boxwood, with points resembling the extremities of the fingers in shape. When the student has had some little practice in manipulating the clay and reproducing simple forms, he should attempt to copy a simple mask—like that of Dante—in which the surfaces are broad, the features large and sharply defined, so that the whole of the work may be done with the thumbs and fingers. These masks, or face, may be obtained at a trifling cost from any figure-moulder.

Monochromatic Drawing.—The board, or material suitable for this drawing, can be purchased at any artist store, either in tinted or plain colors. You need for this painting a knife or eraser, crayons, fine sponge, pencils, cork, rubber, piece of kid, and crayon-holders. Fold several pieces of kid and soft leather, and use in shading the sharp-folded corners; also, double some pieces over the ends of pointed and rounded sticks; the learner will find use for several kinds. Always commence painting with the dark shades, and blend gradually into the light. For very dark shades, rub the crayon directly upon the surface with a light hand, and blend off carefully. Paint the sky first, as in water-colors. It is well to shade distant mountains very light first, and be sure to have the edges soft and faint. For water, scrape some black crayon into powder, and lay it on your board with the kid, working it horizontally, and making the light and shades stronger as it comes nearer. Your sponge may do good in rendering the water transparent. Make sharp lights with the penknife. Ruins overgrown with moss, and dilapidated buildings, may make pretty pictures. We have seen moonlight views, in this style of painting, more beautiful than anything else. Great care should be taken to do the foliage well. Many a picture, which would otherwise have been good, has been spoiled by a stiff, ugly tree. By the delicate use of the round point of a penknife, beautiful effects can be produced in crayon shading. Figures, animals, etc., are put in last; and a person knowing how to shade in pencil will find no difficulty in this.

Moss-Work.—Collecting and arranging, in various forms of

grace and beauty, the delicate and many-colored mosses with which
our fields and forests abound, has long been a favorite pastime with
all lovers of the beautiful in nature. A fertile imagination and inven-
tive mind will readily perceive the many objects for which moss-work
is well adapted. Vases, neatly and tastefully covered with delicate
mosses, arranged with an eye to the harmony of colors, are very ap-
propriate for holding dried grasses; crosses, little towers, "ancient and
moss-grown," for watch-stands; frames for holding collections of leaves,
grasses, or flowers; indeed, it is needless to particularize. Beautiful
landscapes can be made, closely resembling nature.

Collect all the varieties of wood moss, beautiful bits of bark and
dried leaves within your reach. Make a design—perhaps of a landscape—in which are ruins, rocks, etc. Paint a sky, as in water-colors;
then glue thin bits of bark and moss on the ruins; moss on rocks;
dried forest leaves on the distant mountains, and the bright-colored
and green mosses of various hues on the foreground. Such a landscape
is calculated to draw out the ingenuity of the pupil, and requires no
little study, and when well done, is a very pleasant picture. Set in a
deep frame.

Paper Flowers.—Occasionally we see very handsome paper
flowers; but then they are made by persons of taste, with great care,
and from the best of French tissue-paper. Dip a large camel's-hair
pencil in thin gum arabic, and brush quickly over the whole surface
of the paper from which you intend to cut your flower; this fills the
pores of the paper, and gives it a little stiffness. Cut roses, japonicas,
etc., from paper patterns; then paint with water-color. Form the
petal with your fingers and a pair of scissors. Cut a fringe of yellow
paper for stamens. Make your leaves and calyx of green tissue-
paper, well sized with gum. Cover fine well-annealed wire with green
paper for stalks, and fasten the parts of the flower together with gum.
For a daisy, chrysanthemum, or aster, double the paper two or three
times; cut down two thirds; roll the uncut side firmly round and round
the bent end of a piece of wire suitable for the stalk. Buds, pericarps,
etc., are made either by stuffing with a bit of cotton, or winding up
paper. Variegated pinks look well. Paint strips of paper in plashes
here and there, as you see on the petal of the carnation—some very
dark carmine, some merely light touches. Cut off suitable width for
petals, and wind around a paper centre. Take natural flowers for
models.

Imitation Pearl-Work for Embroidery.—We do not
think that a preparation of fish-scales has ever been used in this coun-

try instead of the so-much-admired pearl; and so we give it to our readers, knowing that they will like something entirely new.   Take the shining scales from a carp, or any other fish—the larger the scales the better; put them in strong salt-water over night; lay them on a linen cloth or smooth board; wipe them carefully on both sides, and lay them between clean, strong paper, under a board, on which place a weight; let them remain a day or two, until the scales are pressed dry and become hard.   Draw something, say an ivy-leaf, on strong drawing-paper; cut it out, and lay it on each scale as a pattern, by which to cut the scales with very fine scissors.   Such a pattern, however, is superfluous to persons acquainted with drawing, who can cut leaves of that kind without one.   Vein your scale-leaves with a fine steel needle; do it slowly, bearing on hard to give clearness; the leaves are now ready. · Stretch a rich, dark-colored silk velvet tightly in an embroidery frame; place the pattern which you intend to copy before you, and imitate it by sewing the scale-leaves, one at a time, on the velvet, with fine gold thread, and the leaf-stalks and tendrils embroidered with the same.   It is well to draw the thread through water before using it, to render it flexible.   The beautiful effect produced by this simple process fully repays one for the trouble.   That manifold changes may be made, according to the taste and ingenuity of the copyist, is evident to the reader.

Potchimoni.—Take plain glass jars or vases, in any shape, and clean them thoroughly; then obtain two or three sheets of figures, flowers, or views, in imitation of Chinese, Egyptian, or Swiss painting. These goods, as well as the jars, can be obtained in any of the principal cities.   Now, in whatever style you determine to ornament your vase or jar, cut out the figures from your sheet and secure them in different parts inside the jar, with the figures looking outwards.   The best material for making them adhere is to boil a piece of parchment; this makes a good size.   Having secured the prints, make a varnish of balsam of fir and turpentine, and apply all over inside with a fine brush.   When the first coat is dry, give another coat; now take any color you choose—black, blue, green, yellow, white, pink, brown, or red—and grind the paint fine with the best white varnish, and apply a coat of this paint over the whole inside; let it dry, and then repeat coat upon coat until the color is sufficiently strong to show even and bright outside.   Jars and vases may be decorated in endless variety by this method.   Some use cuttings of prints, silks, etc.

Shell Work.—This is very pretty for vases, frames, boxes, etc. Many shell flowers, animals, birds, and the like, are brought here from the Mediterranean. We have seen some that we would like to own; but in general they have a stiff appearance. However, we will tell you how they are made. Assort your shells according to size and color—the more rice and other small shells you have, the better. Melt white wax and glue together ; two parts of the former and one of the latter. Have a clear idea of what you intend to do; or, what is better, make a pattern before you begin to set your shells. If you will ornament a box, a rose in the centre looks well. Take thin round shells, those most resembling rose-leaves, of the smaller size, and dipping the lower ends in the hot wax mixture, set them close together for the centre of a rose; place other similar-shaped shells around in circles, the largest outward. Care must be taken to form the shells into perfect circles, and to take up wax enough to make them adhere to the cover. Shells of different form, say more oblong, can be used for leaves. After arranging such figures as you like with the shells you have, fill up the spaces with the very small ones. Rice shells are the prettiest, but they are costly. Some prefer sticking the shells into a puttied surface, which does very well. Varnish with a very little copal varnish, using great care.

Etching Shells.—It is done simply by means of acids. The parts not to be acted upon must be protected by a so-called etching-ground, which is nothing but a thin layer of varnish blackened in a flame so as to see plainly the figures afterward drawn on it. Be careful when doing this to make a clear drawing or writing in which the shell is exposed at the bottom of every line, as any remaining varnish would protect those parts, and the writing would not be brought out. The The acid, either strong acetic, diluted nitric, or hydro-chloric, is then applied, and when its action is sufficient it is washed off with water; the varnish is rubbed off with turpentine or alcohol, when the drawing or lettering will appear, and look as if cut with an engraver's tool. You may also make your design with varnish on the shell by means of a fine brush; then the acid will dissolve the surface around the lines drawn, when the writing will appear in relief, the letters being elevated in place of being sunk in, as by the former process. The latter is the more common way in which these shells are treated. This method is applied to many other objects; all that is wanted being a liquid dissolving the material to be acted upon, and a varnish to protect some parts from its action.

Theorem Painting.—This style of painting has been called Oriental Painting, and several other names. It is best adapted to fruits, birds, etc. It enables you to paint on paper, silk, velvet, crape, and light-colored wood..... *To Make Horn Paper.*—Take equal parts mastic and Japan varnish; add to it half as much balsam of fir as there is of either of the varnishes, and a piece of white wax the size of a thimble; simmer together till the wax is melted. If it is too thick, add a little spirits of turpentine. Put it on one side of the paper while it is warm, the paper having previously been prepared with painters' oil, to make it transparent. The oil must be put upon both sides rather warm, and the whole of the paper lie together one night; then wiped with a cloth to absorb the oil on the surface, and dried one week in the sun before varnishing. Each side of the paper must be varnished twice, and the greatest care taken to dry it well. Trace the picture to be copied on white paper with a soft lead pencil, and mark those parts which do not touch each other with a figure 1. Mark another piece of horn paper for theorem 2, and cut again. Thus continue till you have enough theorems for your whole picture. It takes more time to cut a set of theorems nicely than to draw one picture; but a good set of theorems is equal to twenty or thirty sketches, and the durability depends upon the care with which you treat them. You need a brush for every color used; of course, you must have plenty of stiff brushes. Put a few drops of water on your palette with the end of the brush, to avoid dipping the bristles in water. Lay the theorem on the paper to be painted. Good drawing-paper is best for the first attempt. Press the theorem firmly down at each corner with weights, and then proceed to paint. Commence with a leaf; take plenty of paint, a very little moist, on your brush, and paint in the cut leaf of the theorem; hold the brush upright, and work quickly with a circular motion. Commence a little distance from, and work towards, the edges. If you take enough paint, it goes on smoothly; if too much, it looks dauby; if too little, spotted. In shading leaves, cut bits of horn paper on the edge, in the form of large veins, and laying on the leaf already painted, paint from this edge into the leaf. Slip the paper, and paint other veined parts the same way. If successful with leaf, try a grape, which paint first purple, then blue, and finish with carmine. On removing the last of your theorems, if you see any irregularity in the painted parts, lay the theorem on again, and correct; if any spaces, dot in with a fine brush. All fibres, stalks, dots, etc., must be put in with camel's-hair pencils. To heighten the effect, paint may be stuck on here and there with a stiff brush, and the edges blended together to produce softness..... *To Paint on Wood.*—Choose hard wood of light color; paint as above, and varnish when done..... *To Paint on Velvet.*—Use firm white cotton velvet; use paint a little more moistened..... *To Paint on Silk, Satin, and Crape.*—Size the parts to be painted with gum arabic or isinglass, and proceed as with drawing-paper. In this way ball-dresses may be painted with belt and neck-ribbon to match; also, white-crape dresses, with vines of gold and silver.

Transferring to Glass.—Colored or plain engravings, photographs, lithographs, water-colors, oil-colors, crayons, steel plates, newspaper cuts, mezzotints, pencil, writing, show-cards, labels,—or, in fact, anything..... *Directions.*—Take glass that is perfectly clear—window-glass will answer; clean it thoroughly; then varnish it, taking care to have it perfectly smooth ; place it where it will be entirely free from dust; let it stand over night; then take your engraving, lay it in clear water until it is wet through (say ten or fifteen minutes); then lay it upon a newspaper, that the moisture may dry from the surface and still keep the other side damp. Immediately varnish your glass the second time; then place your engraving on it, pressing it down firmly, so as to exclude every particle of air; next rub the paper from the back until it is of uniform thickness—so t_in that you can see through it; then varnish it the third time, and let it dry..... *Materials used for the above art.*—Take two ounces balsam of fir to one ounce of spirits of turpentine; apply with a camel's-hair brush.

Transferring to Wood.—Dissolve salt in soft water; float your engraving on the surface, picture side up; let it remain about one hour. Your screen-box or table should be of bird's-eye maple, or other light-colored hard wood; varnish with best copal or transfer varnish. Take the picture from the water; dry a little between linen rags; then put the engraving, picture side down, on the varnished wood, and smooth it nicely. If the picture entirely covers the wood after the margin is cut off, so that no varnish be exposed, lay over it a thin board and heavy weight; leave it thus in press over night. If you wish but a small picture in the centre of your wood, apply the varnish only to a space the size of your picture. Dip your forefinger in salt and water, and commence with rubbing off the paper; the nearer you come to the engraving, the more careful you must be, as a hole would spoil your work. Rub slowly and patiently till you have taken off every bit of the paper, and left only the black lines and touches of your picture on the wood, in an inverted direction. Finish up with two or three coats of copal varnish.

To Make Transparencies.—Take some prettily colored landscape, and cut a slit into the broad lights of it with a penknife; put a white paper of medium thickness behind it, and interline with orange or rose-colored paper; bind the three—that is, the landscape, the colored paper, and the paper which forms the back—together with some suitable color for a frame; now separate the cut edges of your landscape by pressing them apart. Hang up in the window, and when the sun shines through, the effect is beautiful. Try it; we are sure you will be pleased.

An engraving prepared as for Grecian painting is very pretty for a screen, or to hang in the window. Lamp-shades may be made in this way, and many pretty designs will suggest themselves—bouquets, wreaths, vines running round the shade, etc. Also, still more beautiful is the antique style, before painting.

To Prepare Butterflies for Collections.—The first thing to be procured is the butterfly-net, which is a bag made out of two pieces of mosquito-netting—blue is the best—about two feet deep, tapering towards the bottom, and fastened to a piece of stout wire bent into a circle of about a foot in diameter, the two ends of which are fastened into a light but strong stick three or four feet in length.

The next requisite is something to kill them with. Chloroform is best, but in default of that ether will do. It should be applied to the head of the butterfly with a small camel's-hair brush.

Then come the pins. They should be long and slender; real butterfly pins are best, but very fine common ones will do. Then you must have a pasteboard box to put the butterflies in when you catch them to bring them home.

The cases are the last thing to be thought of. The frame of the case should be very much like a picture frame, deep enough for the pins to go in, with the back, on which the butterflies are fastened, so arranged as to come out, being held in place by little cleats, and a plate of glass fixed securely on the front. It should be made of soft wood, so that the pins can stick in easily. The size of the case depends upon the taste of the collector. .

"Stretching" a butterfly is the process of keeping its wings in the natural position when at rest. You should have a board with grooves in it wide enough to admit the body of the butterfly or moth, with little pieces of cork fastened on it to stick the pins into. Then take some narrow strips of soft paper, press the wings of the butterfly down with them as nearly in the natural position as possible, and fasten them with pins. In a few days the butterfly will be dry enough so you can take the papers off and put it in the case.

Crayon Drawing.—Drawing in crayon will be found much more convenient than in oil or water colors, as you are spared the delay of waiting for them to dry. Crayon materials or pastels are put up in boxes of necessary tints for portraits or landscapes, and, by blending, every shade and color can be obtained as in oil painting. The pupil can purchase prepared paper or board. A good paper for portraiture is pumice paper. Your sketch should be made as in penciling, and then proceed to the shading. For a head, we consider the drapery and groundwork—and here allow me to advise all to study penciling before attempting crayons; also, to begin by painting easy things. The picture being drawn, proceed to fill in the background. Let the tints be varied, if in a colored crayon, according to the ideal or originals from which you are designing it. For example, if the lights in your picture are on the right side, the darkest shade in the groundwork must be placed on the right, and *vice versa*. See that the background be smooth, the dark shades of rich brown or green, and the light of gray, French blue, etc. Then—

1. Paint the dark shades with black crayon, and rub it in with a soft cork. The cork pencils ready prepared are best for that purpose, or rubbers of soft leather will answer.

2. Put in the light clear shades as they belong with the soft and medium crayons, using care in blending to avoid a dingy and dirty appearance.

3. Lay on the brown and other colors. When it is necessary to put brown over black, do not rub the two together; use your finger, as well as the cork.

4. In finishing the picture use hard crayon, laying on in lines, and blend with cork.

Having a variety of colors for other styles of painting, you can use your judgment in selecting from your boxes. You must have a box of soft and a box of hard crayons to obtain what you need. Try your colors first on a piece of waste paper. Do not expect it will be right by laying on colors, once. You must work line over line many times and carefully. Do not soil your picture in the delicate parts. In addition to your colors in boxes, furnish yourself with black and white crayons of different tones, and a supply of dry carmine. We prefer the lump to the pencil. French blue is much used to produce clear lights. The paper must be some available tint, as its color appears through almost all portions of the work. A low-toned olive tint has been found very desirable. Have your paper an inch or two longer than the proposed picture; sketch the design lightly with black crayon No. 1, making sky and broad tints with the flat surface of broken pieces of crayon (1 and 2) rubbed in with the finger. The breadths of the nearer and remote distances are put in with broken pieces, blended together. Mountains, trees, etc., are drawn in with black crayon, then tinted and glazed with colored crayon.

Simple Method of Copying Drawings.—Silvered albumen paper, after being washed, may be conveniently used for copying negatives as well as positives. It keeps for weeks, and becomes sensitive to light only after exposure to the vapors of aqua ammonia, technically termed "smoking with ammonia." Dr. H. Vogel has greatly simplified the latter process by substituting for the liquid ammonia the powder of carbonate of ammonia. He thoroughly impregnates a piece of felt or cloth with this powder, and lays it under the silvered sheet, separated from it by a piece of blotting-paper. The negative is placed on the top, and the back covered, and the whole is ready for the copying frame. One impregnation with the carbonate of ammonia serves for several copies. So very simple is the operation that Dr. Vogel has made use of it in public libraries for copying complicated drawings. He places the silvered paper, with the substratum of carbonate of ammonia and the drawing on top, between two plates of glass, and exposing it to the light of the window, obtains a copy quite distinct in all its details, while he himself may be occupied with reading or otherwise. The copy obtained is, of course, in white lines upon black ground. Such photographs merely require to be treated with soda when intended for long preservation. They are generally, however, not designed to be kept a great while.

Photograph Coloring.—Select a light photograph for coloring, and let the general hue be gray, inclining to black in the shadows.

Albumenized paper seldom requires any preparation, but need only be carefully washed with cold water and a soft sponge.

A preparation of gum is generally used in the colors for albumen paper. It should be dissolved in water, or allowed to boil up; after which, bottle to keep from dust.

A little white sugar is added by some artists; and the preparation should be used as thin as possible and allow the colors to adhere readily to the paper.

The following colors are necessary in cakes. Windsor and Newton's being considered the best:—Carmine, vermilion, rose madder, light red, crimson lake, Roman ochre, Indian yellow, gamboge, cobalt blue, emerald green, indigo, Prussian blue, burnt sienna, burnt umber, sepia, Van Dyke brown, madder brown, ivory black, Chinese white, (half cakes at half price).

Sable brushes are best, and should not be used too small, except for delicate work, such as marking in the eyes, nostrils, etc. A middling size is preferable, but see that there are no straggling hairs about them and that they do not split or divide.

Coloring the Face—Commence, with large brush, to wash in the flesh tint: go over the whole flesh as smoothly as possible; light red is the most desirable, being a fast color; for very fair complexions orange vermilion is used.

Put pale wash of cobalt blue in the half tints, Indian yellow in dark shadows, with vermilion and carmine (mixed) over it.

After the washes in the face, put in the hair, draperies, background, etc.

Stipple the whole flesh with tints of light red, or Indian yellow and pink madder mixed.

Stipple rose madder on cheeks, lips, tip of the chin, tip of ears and over the nose where the eyes meet; cobalt blue in temples and about the shadows of the eyes and mouth.

Stipple light tint of Indian yellow over the cheek bones; in faces of old persons more Indian yellow is used; also in faces of brunettes.

A pale green, made of Indian yellow and cobalt blue, is sometimes used in shadows about the mouth.

Sepia or Van Dyke brown for brown hair.

Shade with sepia and carmine, and use cobalt blue mixed with burnt sienna for high lights.

Pale wash of cobalt blue on high lights of black hair, and shade with black and carmine.

Roman ochre for golden hair, with burnt sienna and cobalt blue in lights; shade with sepia and Roman ochre.

For gray hair mix a wash of cobalt blue and sepia; shadow with sepia; and sometimes use white mixed with local color for high lights.

Backgrounds.—For fair complexions or children should be blue, inclining to purple. Cobalt blue and burnt umber make very desirable backgrounds.

Olive grounds are used for dark or old complexions. Where the flesh tint is sallow, use warmer colors—green approaching to olive.

Grays produce a pleasing effect on fair complexions.

Never paint a bright blue ground and crimson curtains, but keep everything quiet and subdued.

Opaque backgrounds are far from artistic, and but seldom used.

Stippling.—Towards the end of your work you will observe many inequalities in the tints. These require to be filled up with the point of a brush with an assimilating color; and that filling up is termed stippling.

Draperies.—For black draperies. first use a local wash of ivory black; wash in the deep shadows with a mixture of crimson lake and sepia; then add another wash of black over the whole, touching in the shadows as before. Proceed in this way for two or three washes, and then touch in the high lights with light red and white.

Tinting Photographs Slightly.—Having prepared the photograph in the usual way, take a little pink madder or carmine, and lay it on the cheek with a clean pencil. Soften it carefully all round the edges, blending the tint into the face. Repeat the process once and again, until you have obtained nearly as much color as necessary; I say nearly as much, because you have to pass the general flesh wash over it, which has the effect of darkening it considerally. For the purpose of softening, it will be as well to have two pencils on one holder. It might appear that putting on the color of the cheek at once, and softening it, would suffice; but you will get it far softer by doing it with a very pale tint two or three times, than you possibly can by making it at once as powerful as necessary; besides, it is impossible to soften a strong color so well as a pale tint. When the color is quite dry, go over the whole of the face with a flesh tint, then put in the hair, eyes, eyebrows, and lips; round off the forehead with gray, and apply the same to those parts of the face where you observe it to be in nature. If your photograph be a very dark one, you will not require so much gray in it as if it were a light impression. Next wash in the background and proceed with the draperies, etc.

Return now to the face; strengthen the carnations, grays, and shadows, by hatching delicate tints over them; put the light in the eyes, and the spirited touches about it, and the eyebrows, mouth, etc., and finish off the hair. In dark photographs, you will require to lay the lights on the hair with body color, as it is generally much darker than it appears in nature. Make out the linen with a gray, deepening it in the darkest parts, and lay on the high lights with constant or Chinese white. Proceed next to shadow the drapery, and when you have obtained the required depth, scumble in the high lights, using a bare pencil and a very gentle hand, as before directed. Give the background another wash, if requisite, and your photograph is finished; or make up a tint of orange vermilion and white, according to the complexion, and lay it smoothly over face and hands; then put on the carnations with rose madder, and shadow up the face with orange tint, and proceed as above to finish. If the backgrounds and draperies appear dead, you may take a piece of very soft washing silk and rub them up a little, which will have the same effect as if they had been hot pressed. Whenever body color has been used, the rubbing will be ineffective. Neither rubbing nor hot pressing will give a shine to any but transparent tints. If there be metal buttons, chains, or epaulettes, they must be laid over the dress with body colors; a very good ground for them is red chrome and gamboge, shadowed with burnt umber, and heightened on the lights with lemon chrome and Chinese white. By the foregoing methods, it will be unnecessary to hatch or stipple a great deal; for you will find that the face will come out very soft and round without it, but the effect is far inferior to that produced by the other process.

Painting Flowers in Water Colors.—The colors and materials requisite are carmine, crimson lake, cobalt blue, Prussian blue, vermilion, gamboge, raw sienna, burnt sienna, burnt umber, Chinese white, yellow ochre, and Indian ink—a set of saucers, dissolved gum arabic, and a few sable brushes, Rose pink, royal scarlet, Indian yellow, Indian red, indigo, sepia, Van Dyke brown, and emerald green, may also be added for flowers of superior finish.

Whatman's hot-pressed paper, stretched on a board, as in landscape painting, is used to good advantage. Bush flowers are generally painted on London board, the ivory surface sometimes preferred. Make an accurate and clean sketch with fine pointed pencil, drawing the marks faint, so as not to use rubber often. When sketched, moisten all parts intended for painting with a brush moderately filled with water. Never use hard water, unless it has been boiled. This prepares the paper to receive the colors. Some use a slight shade of neutral tint or Indian ink to coat over the shaded parts, blending the shades so that they are imperceptibly lost. Flowers and leaves are treated the same. Two brushes are used, one charged with color, the other nearly dry. After this process, cast with local color, finish with soft washes or small touches, which is called stippling, and, when done nicely, is beautiful; but as it takes time, washes are more generally adopted. Practice will accustom the eye to notice variety of shades, which before could not be discriminated.

Green leaves, when a yellowish pale green and bright, are painted with gamboge and a little Prussian blue, penciled over until the effect is obtained. Use more Prussian blue for darker green leaves, finishing with stronger color. For the deepest shades, add a little crimson lake, or Van Dyke brown, or burnt sienna; as the shade requires. For decayed leaves, use burnt sienna, Indian yellow; and crimson lake.

Yellow Flowers. First examine whether the shades are warm or cool: if the latter, paint them with Indian ink; if the former, use a little burnt umber. When dry, coat evenly with gamboge—the general tint of the flower. Where the high lights should be, wash out a little with another brush while it is moist. Repeat the color in the stronger parts, finishing, if requisite, with a little carmine or burnt sienna mixed with gamboge.

Blue Flowers. Coat them evenly with cobalt, according to tint. A little rose madder added to cobalt may be used, as the tints should vary. Shade the deeper parts with a little Prussian blue added to it; and if a very deep tint is required, add a little indigo.

Purple Flowers. Make the desired tint with carmine and Prussian blue, increasing the shade to the depth required, using more color and less water.

Scarlet Flowers. Paint the shades in with cobalt blue and a little Indian red; then coat smoothly with royal scarlet, or carmine and gamboge mixed, finishing up with carmine on the shades. If coated with royal scarlet, add carmine in finishing.

White Flowers. Some are first shaded with Indian ink, and others with neutral tint, made of cobalt, rose madder, and Indian yellow.— When dry, slightly tint some of the petals with a weak shade of yellow ochre, some parts with cobalt, others with a greenish neutral. The anthers, if not left white, should be done with permanent white added to Indian yellow, and carefully dotted with weak burnt sienna.

The Deep Crimson Rose. Shade all the petals more or less with Indian ink, until it would pass for a finished drawing in Indian ink, and then coat twice with strong carmine, finishing deep shades with a little Prussian blue added to carmine.

Pink Rose. Paint in the shades with cobalt blue, and coat over with a pale shade of carmine, with a little vermilion added. Repeat this on some of the petals, until the requisite depth is obtained. Some of the outside petals may need a second coat of cobalt to give them a thin, transparent appearance.

Arranging and Grouping. With those who possess a good eye for color, the most pleasing arrangements easily suggest themselves. Sometimes the most pleasing effects are obtained by placing the light flowers in the center, such as pink, white, and pale yellows, placing the rich dark colors outside, such as dark roses, etc., thereby making a substitute for light and shade. The most pleasing groups are painted with a predominance of warm coloring.

Good Books Mailed on Receipt of Price.

Preserving and Manufacturing Secrets.—This book gives plain directions for preserving, canning, and storing all kinds of fruits and vegetables, and for manufacturing all kinds of foreign and domestic liquors, home-made wines and summer beverages. It gives a new, simple and cheap plan of preserving eggs fresh for five years (if necessary), so that when opened they will taste as if freshly laid. This receipt alone has often been sold for $5. It tells housekeepers how to make all varieties of palatable and delicious fruit jellies and jams. It shows how to make a fruity and sweet tasting cider without apples that when bottled will foam and effervesce like genuine champagne. It tells how to keep fruit and vegetables fresh all the year round. All about pickling. How to make all kinds of liquors at home at a trifling expense, and which cannot be told from that sold at $5 to $10 a gallon, etc., etc. Mailed for only 50 cents.

Secrets for Farmers.—This book tells how to restore rancid butter to its original flavor and purity ; a new way of coloring butter ; how largely to increase the milk of cows ; a sure cure for kicking cows ; how to make Thorley's celebrated condimental food for cattle ; how to make hens lay every day in the year ; it gives an effectual remedy for the Canada thistle ; to save mice girded trees ; a certain plan to destroy the curculo and peach borer ; how to convert dead animals and bones into manure ; Barnet's certain preventive for the potato rot, worth $50 to any farmer ; remedy for smut in wheat ; to cure blight in fruit-trees ; to destroy the potato bug ; to prevent mildew and rust in wheat ; to destroy the cut worm : home-made stump machine, as good as any sold ; to keep cellars from freezing, etc., etc. It is impossible to give the full contents of this very valuable book here, space will not allow. It will be mailed for 30 cents.

The Housewife's Treasure.—A manual of information of everything that relates to household economies. It gives the method of making Jackson's Universal Washing Compound, which will clean the dirtiest cotton, linen or woolen cloths in twenty minutes without rubbing or harming the material. This receipt is being constantly peddled through the country at $5 each, and is certainly worth it. It also tells all about soap-making at home, so as to make it cost about one-quarter of what bar-soap costs ; it tells how to make candles by moulding or dipping ; it gives seven methods for destroying rats and mice ; how to make healthy bread without flour (something entirely new) ; to preserve clothes and furs from moths ; a sure plan of destroying house flies, cockroaches, beetles, ants, bed-bugs and fleas ; all about house-cleaning, papering, etc., etc., and hundreds of other valuable hints just such as housekeepers are wanting to know. Mailed for 30 cents.

Educating the Horse.—A new and improved system of educating the horse. Also a treatise on shoeing, with new and valuable receipts for diseases of horses, together with the Rules of the Union Course. This book contains matter not to be found in any other work on the horse. Mailed for 25 cents.

Our Boys' and Girls' Favorite Speaker.—Containing patriotic, Sentimental, Poetical, and Comic Gems of Oratory, by Chapin, Dickens, Dow, Jr., Beecher, Burns, Artemus Ward, Everett, Tennyson, Webster, and others. Mailed for 20 cents.

The Common-Sense Cook-Book.—Showing fully what to eat and how to cook it. Mailed for 20 cents.

Address   **FRANK M. REED,**

139 Eighth Street, New York.

A new book showing how to Acquire and Retain Bodily Symmetry, Health, Vigor, and Beauty. Its contents are as follows : Laws of Beauty—Air, Sunshine, Water, and Food—Work and Rest—Dress and Ornament—The Hair and its Management—Skin and Complexion—the Mouth—The Eyes, Ears and Nose—The Neck, Hands, and Feet—Growth and Marks that are Enemies of Beauty—Cosmetics and Perfumery.

Fat People.—It gives ample rules how Corpulency may be Cured—the Fat made Lean, Comely and Active.

Lean People.—It also gives directions, the following of which will enable Lean, Angular, Bony or Sharp Visaged People, to be Plump and Rosy Skinned.

Gray Hair.—It tells how Gray Hair may be Restored to its natural color without the aid of Dyes, Restorers, or Pomades.

Baldness.—It gives ample directions for Restoring Hair on Bald Heads, as well as how to stop Falling of the Hair, how to Curl the Hair, etc.

Beard and Mustache.—It tells what Young Men should do to acquire a Fine Silky and Handsome Beard and Mustache.

Freckles and Pimples.—It gives full directions for the Cure of Sunburn, Freckles, Pimples, Wrinkles, Warts, etc., so that they can be entirely removed.

Cosmetics.—This chapter, among other things, gives an Analysis of Perry's Moth and Freckle Lotion, Balm of White Lilies, Hagan's Magnolia Balm, Laird's Bloom of Youth, Phalon's Enamel, Clark's Restorative for the Hair, Chevalier's Life for the Hair, Ayer's Hair Vigor, Professor Wood's Hair Restorative, Hair Restorer America, Gray's Hair Restorative, Phalon's Vitalia, Ring's Vegetable Ambrosia, Mrs. Allen's World's Hair Restorer, Hall's Vegetable Sicilian Hair Renewer, Martha Washington Hair Restorative, etc., etc. (no room for more), showing how the lead, etc., in these mixtures cause disease and oftentimes premature death. Mailed for 50 cents.

The Management and Care of Infants and Children.—By Geo. Combe, M.D. This is the best book ever written on the subject, and is one that no mother of a family can afford to be without Its usual price in the book stores is $1.50, but it will be mailed—*the latest and most complete edition*—for only 75 cents.

Address   **FRANK M. REED,**

139 Eighth Street, New York.

www.ingramcontent.com/pod-product-compliance
Lightning Source LLC
Chambersburg PA
CBHW020818030726
47496CB00009B/2948